the Great Monarch Butterfly Chase

To Irene, my love and inspiration
—R.W.N.P.

For my aunt, Rebecca Epstein
—B.G.

Bradbury Press
Macmillan Publishing Company
866 Third Avenue
New York, NY 10022

Maxwell Macmillan Canada, Inc.
1200 Eglinton Avenue East
Suite 200
Don Mills, Ontario M3C 3N1

Macmillan Publishing Company is part of the Maxwell Communication Group of Companies.

First edition
Printed and bound in Hong Kong by South China Printing Company (1988) Ltd.
10 9 8 7 6 5 4 3 2 1
The text of this book is set in Souvenir Gothic Light.

LIBRARY OF CONGRESS CATALOGING-IN-PUBLICATION DATA
Prior, R. W. N.
The great monarch butterfly chase / by R.W.N. Prior, illustrated by Beth Glick.
p.   cm.
Summary: Jason and Tommy follow a monarch butterfly on his migratory flight from the northern United States to Mexico.
ISBN 0-02-775145-7
[1. Monarch butterfly—Fiction.   2. Butterflies—Fiction.]
I. Glick, Beth, ill.   II. Title.
PZ7.P9375Gr   1993
[Fic]—dc20   92-7423

the Great Monarch Butterfly Chase

by *R.W.N. Prior*

illustrated by *Beth Glick*

BRADBURY PRESS
New York

Maxwell Macmillan Canada
Toronto
Maxwell Macmillan International
New York   Oxford   Singapore   Sydney

"This is the laziest day of the year," said Jason.
"What can we do today?" asked Tommy.

The boys looked around and saw some
butterflies in a garden.

"What does a butterfly do all day?" wondered Jason.

"Let's follow one and find out," Tommy answered.

They chose a beautiful monarch butterfly to follow.

"Not too close," said Jason.

The monarch butterfly flew to the goldenrod,

and then to the milkweed,

then across to a field of wildflowers.
Jason and Tommy ran after it.

"Faster," said Jason.
The boys could barely keep up
as the monarch flew across town.

Over the park

and over the zoo,

the monarch flew higher and higher.
Up, up, up, to almost one mile high.
Jason and Tommy chased the butterfly

down through New York State to New York City,

across Washington, D.C.,

CANADA

UNITED STATES

MEXICO

GULF of MEXICO

ATLANTIC OCEAN

through the South and along the Gulf of Mexico.

Then the monarch butterfly landed in Texas

and ate and ate until it could barely move.

But then it flew again,
and the boys followed

all the way to Mexico,

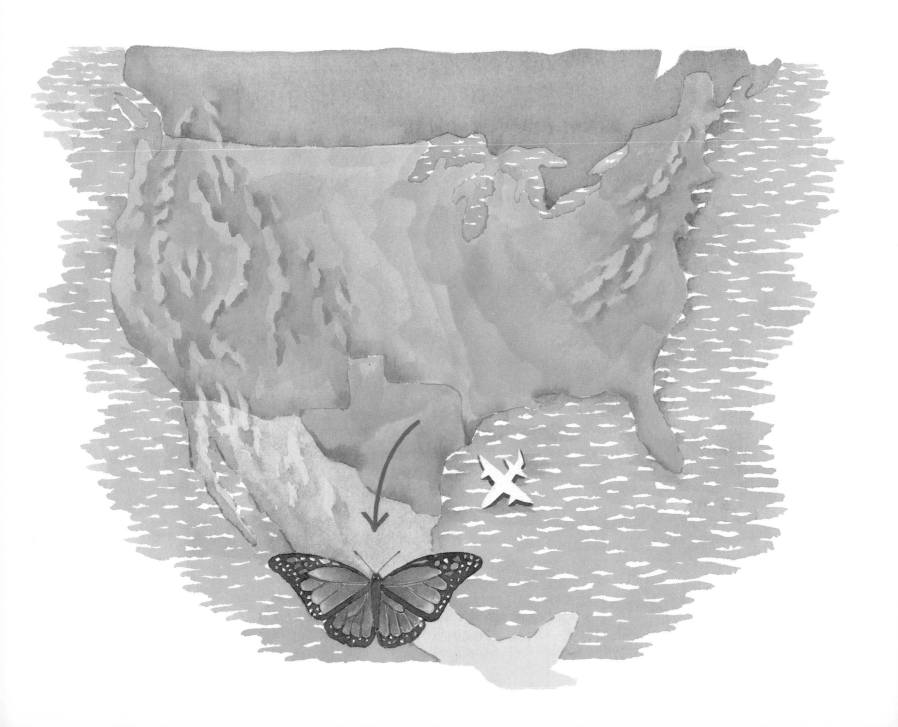

to a small town called Toluca.

Jason and Tommy could barely keep up
as the monarch flew up a mountainside,
higher and higher,
ten thousand feet up the mountain,

to a forest filled with trees called sacred firs.

There the boys saw their butterfly join
another monarch, and another,

and then they saw over
one million butterflies in the fir trees.

Jason and Tommy knew that the
monarch butterfly was finally home.

MORE ABOUT THE MONARCH BUTTERFLY

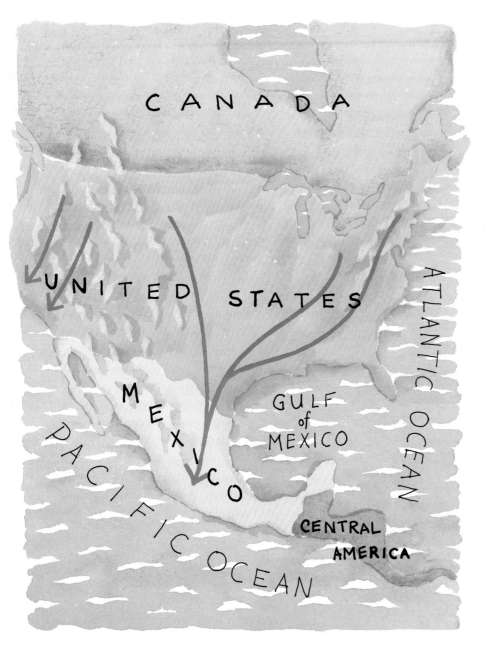

Monarch caterpillars are hatched on milkweed plants all over the United States and southern Canada during spring and summer.

Monarch butterflies cannot survive cold temperatures. So, beginning in mid-September, they begin their flight south. Scientists think that fewer hours of daylight and cooler night temperatures are two things that tell the monarchs it is time to move.

Monarch butterflies living west of the Rocky Mountains fly to California for the winter. The monarchs living east of the Rockies fly to Mexico. The two places have climates that are very similar during the winter.

The butterflies stop to drink nectar from wildflowers for energy for their journey. When they get close to where they will spend the winter, they drink a lot of nectar to store as food for the coming months.

Some of the autumn wildflowers monarchs feed from during their flight can be grown in flower gardens. Goldenrod, aster, boneset, joe-pye weed, purple coneflower, yellow sage, and Japanese privet are flowers that attract monarch butterflies.